BIOGRAPHIES OF DIVERSE HEROES

MALALA YOUSAFZAI

STEPHANIE GASTON

TABLE OF CONTENTS

A Crabtree Seedlings Book

School-to-Home Support for Caregivers and Teachers

This book helps children grow by letting them practice reading. Here are a few guiding questions to help the reader with building his or her comprehension skills. Possible answers appear here in red.

Before Reading:

- What do I think this book is about?
  - *I think this book is about the life of a hero named Malala Yousafzai.*
  - *I think this book will describe the strong character and accomplishments of Malala Yousafzai.*

- What do I want to learn about this topic?
  - *I want to learn what inspired young Malala to speak out against the fierce Taliban rule in Pakistan.*
  - *I want to learn how Malala was able to be brave after being shot in the head.*

During Reading:

- I wonder why...
  - *I wonder why the Taliban began closing schools for girls in Malala Yousafzai's hometown.*
  - *I wonder why Malala would return to Pakistan after being shot there even though it was to receive an award.*

- What have I learned so far?
  - *I have learned that in 2020 Malala graduated from the University of Oxford in England.*
  - *I have learned that she continues to be an advocate for education.*

After Reading:

- What details did I learn about this topic?
  - *I have learned that Malala Yousafzai started her foundation the Malala Fund to promote education for every girl.*
  - *I have learned that Malala became the youngest person ever to win the Nobel Peace Prize at the age of 17.*

- Read the book again and look for the glossary words.
  - *I see the word **Taliban** on page 6 and the word **injustice** on page 8. The other glossary words are found on page 22.*

MALALA YOUSAFZAI

Malala Yousafzai is an education **advocate** and an inspiration to girls around the world.

Malala was born in Pakistan on July 12, 1997.

Her father was an educator who founded the Khushal school, which Malala attended.

Khushal school that Malala used to attend

In 2007, the **Taliban** took over Malala's town and began closing schools for girls.

They also **enforced** harsh punishments and banned many activities.

School destroyed by the Taliban

Malala was only 11 years old when she spoke out publicly against the **injustice**.

Malala then began writing about life under Taliban rule.

Malala's writing gained unwanted attention from the Taliban.

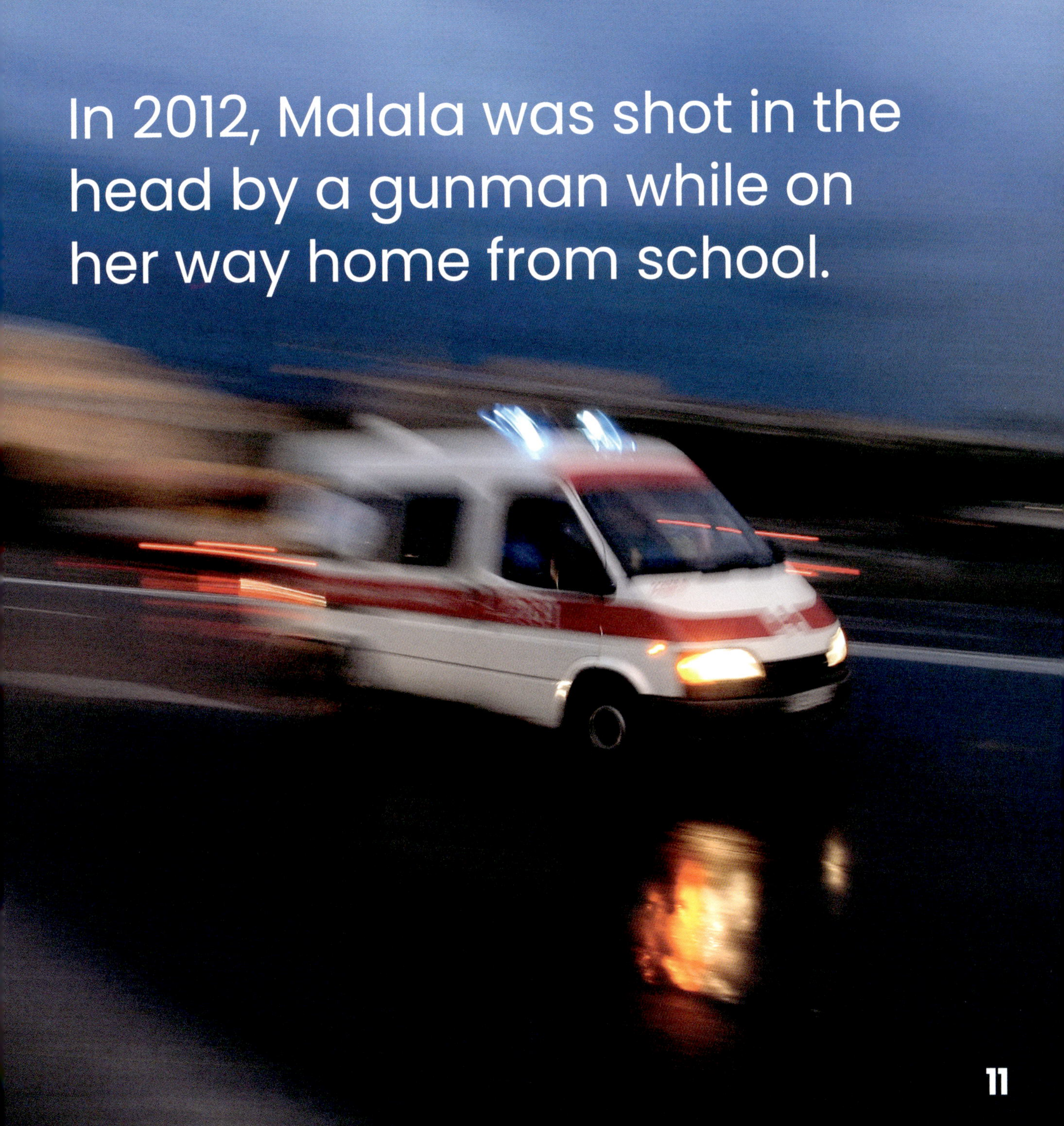

In 2012, Malala was shot in the head by a gunman while on her way home from school.

Miraculously, Malala survived the attack and fully recovered after months in the hospital.

She moved with her family to live in the United Kingdom.

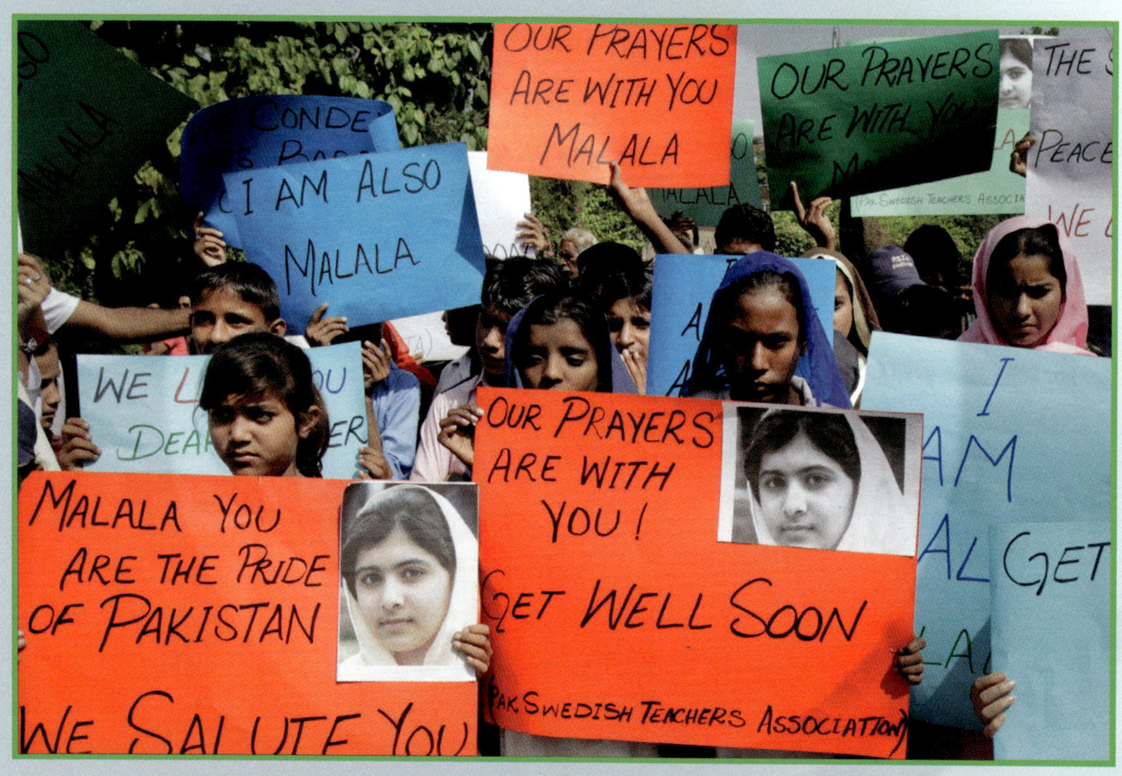

In 2018, Malala returned to Pakistan for the first time since the Taliban attack.

She was being honored for her work as an advocate for education.

In 2020, Malala graduated from the University of Oxford in England.

She earned one of the school's most **prestigious** degrees.

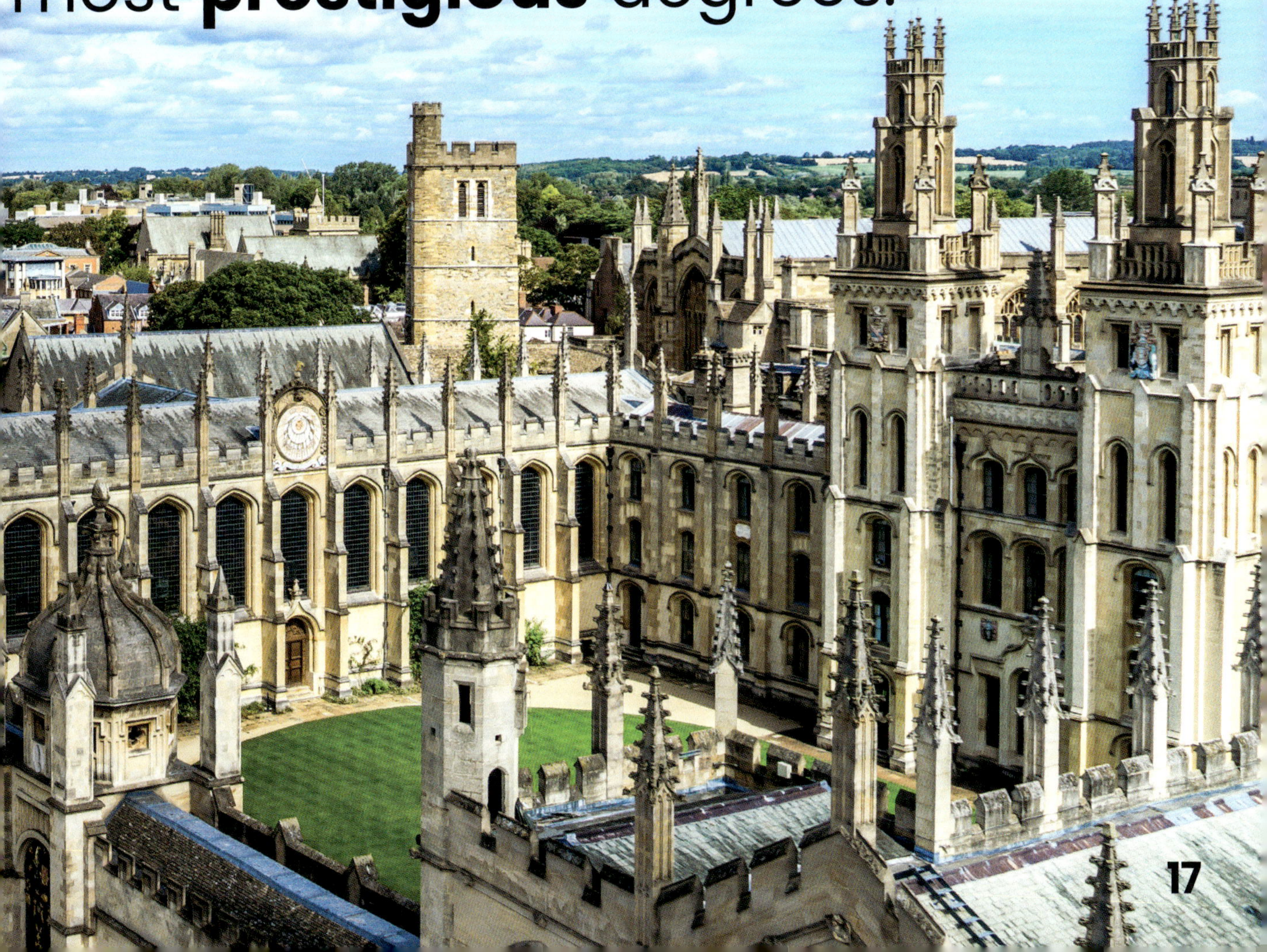

Malala continues to fight for education through her foundation, the Malala Fund.

The mission is to ensure every girl is given the opportunity to achieve a bright future.

Malala became the youngest person ever to win the **Nobel Peace Prize** at the age of 17.

Malala is also the second Pakistani to win the Nobel Peace Prize.

Glossary

advocate (ad-vuh-keyt): A person who speaks up and argues in favor of a person or cause

enforced (en-fawrsd): To force or demand obedience

injustice (in-juhs-tis): Behavior or treatment that is not fair or lawful

Nobel Peace Prize (noh-bel pees prahyz): Award made annually for outstanding achievement in the promotion of peace

prestigious (pre-stee-juhs): Inspiring respect and admiration

Taliban (tal-uh-ban): A Muslim extremist group

Index

"One child, one teacher, one book, one pen can change the world."

—Malala Yousafzai

About the Author

Stephanie Gaston is a content producer for CNN and a screenwriter. She spent more than a decade working for the FOX and ABC affiliates in Miami, Florida, before joining the ranks at CNN in 2015, ahead of an unprecedented election cycle. Stephanie is a first-generation Haitian American who grew up in Fort Lauderdale, Florida, a diverse community with Latin and Caribbean influences. Throughout her career in journalism, Stephanie has covered major stories including presidential inaugurations, natural disasters, and royal weddings. Stephanie is a dog lover, movie buff, fitness enthusiast, and most importantly, a proud mom.

Written by: Stephanie Gaston
Designed by: Under the Oaks Media
Proofreader: Petrice Custance
Print coordinator: Katherine Berti

Photographs: Simon Davis: cover; Zuma Press: p. 3; Reuters: p. 5, 12, 21; Asianet Pakistan: p. 6; Shark9208888: p. 7; Trent Inness: p. 8; razum: p. 9; Svetlana Turchenick: p. 10; logoboom: p. 11; Gorodenkoff: p. 12-13; Punnawit Suwattananun: p. 15; Alicia Vera for Malala Fund: p. 15(b); gowithstock: p. 16-17; Malin Fezehai for Malala Fund

Library and Archives Canada Cataloguing in Publication

Available at the Library and Archives Canada

Library of Congress Cataloging-in-Publication Data

Available at the Library of Congress

Crabtree Publishing Company

www.crabtreebooks.com 1-800-387-7650

In Canada: We acknowledge the financial support of the Government of Canada through the Canada Book Fund for our publishing activities.

Published in the United States
Crabtree Publishing
347 Fifth Avenue
Suite 1402-145
New York, NY, 10016

Published in Canada
Crabtree Publishing
616 Welland Ave.
St. Catharines, ON
L2M 5V6

Printed in the U.S.A./072022/CG20220201